For my three little builders—
sketch a dream and go, go, go for it!

-M.F.

For Jenna

-J.

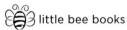 little bee books

An imprint of Bonnier Publishing USA
251 Park Avenue South, New York, NY 10010
Text copyright © 2017 by Meg Fleming
Illustrations copyright © 2017 by Jarvis
All rights reserved, including the right of reproduction in whole or in part in any form.
LITTLE BEE BOOKS is a trademark of Bonnier Publishing USA, and associated
colophon is a trademark of Bonnier Publishing USA.
Manufactured in China   HH 0617
First Edition   10 9 8 7 6 5 4 3 2
Identifiers: LCCN 2015049766 | ISBN 9781499801750 (hardcover)
Library of Congress Cataloging-in-Publication Data
Names: Fleming, Meg, author. | Jarvis, Peter, 1985- illustrator.
Title: Ready, Set, Build! / by Meg Fleming ; illustrated by Peter Jarvis.
Description: New York : little bee books, [2017] | Summary: A builder sketches a project,
then gets to work with his friend, digging, lifting, and sawing.
Subjects: | CYAC: Stories in rhyme. | Building—Fiction. | Friendship—Fiction.
Classification: LCC PZ8.3.F639 Re 2017 | DDC [E]—dc23
LC record available at https://lccn.loc.gov/2015049766

littlebeebooks.com
bonnierpublishingusa.com

READY, SET, BUILD!

WORDS
by
MEG
FLEMING

PICTURES
by
JARVIS

little bee books

Grab your hard hat,　　　**tie your boots.**

Pack your lunch.

Ready? Scoot!

Sketch a dream. Post a chart.

Hatch the plan before you start.

Move the rubble. Clear the space.
Setting up is half the race.

Guide the backhoe off the rig.
Check the ground before you dig.

Keep your head up. Stay on track.

Use your legs and not your back.

Lift together, "1 – 2 – 3!"

Break for lunch beneath a tree.

Goggles on before you slice.
Cut just once—but measure twice.

. . . plug your ears!

Saw blades scream and hammers crack!
Cranes construct a tower stack.

Easy does it on the lift.

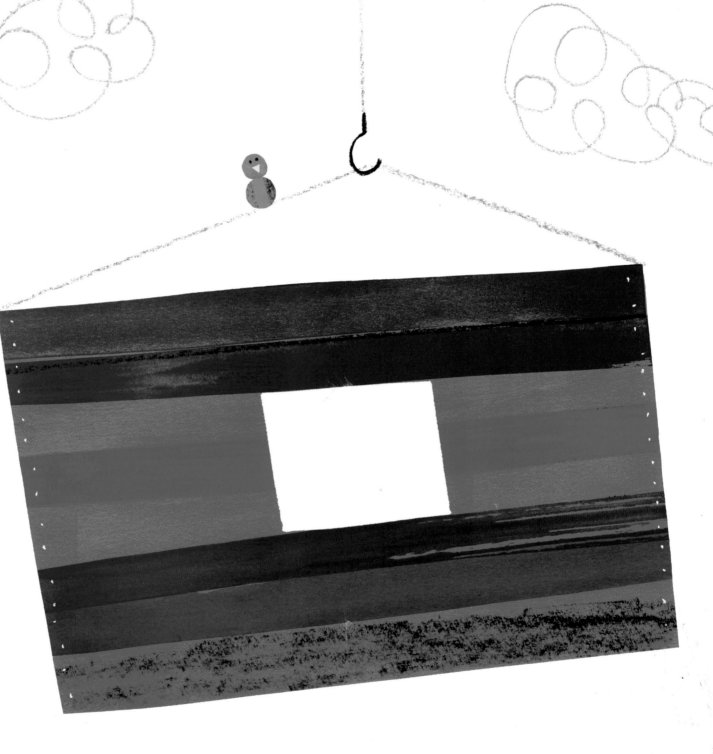

Buckle up, so you don't shift.

Windows in and shingles ready?

Seal the roof and come down steady.

Take a look. Enjoy your view.

Sun goes home and so can you.

Hang your hard hat. Job well done.

Tomorrow's work . . .

. . . is twice the fun!